GIBBY'S
BALL

AuthorHouse™
1663 Liberty Drive
Bloomington, IN 47403
www.authorhouse.com
Phone: 833-262-8899

ISBN: 979-8-8230-1194-5 (sc)
ISBN: 979-8-8230-1195-2 (e)

Library of Congress Control Number: 2023913816

Print information available on the last page.

Published by AuthorHouse 07/25/2023

author HOUSE®

I grew up in Los Angeles, the City of Angels. As a child we lived in a mostly Hispanic neighborhood just a few miles from Chavez Ravine, home of my all-time favorite sports team. In my house we bled Blue and from the beginning of April until late October, if the baseball Gods deemed us worthy, it was all Dodgers all the time. My room was painted Dodger Blue, adorned with pennants, bobble heads, and photographs of my favorite players, many of them signed. Orel Hershiser hung out there. Next to him was Mike Scioscia. John Shelby occupied a prominent spot on the far wall right next to Fernando Valenzuela. I even had some of the old timers. Ron Cey, the Steves; Garvey and Yeager, Dusty Baker, and Rick Monday. But my all-time favorite memento was an autographed poster of Kirk Gibson, arm in mid cock, as he rounded the bases after hitting probably the most famous home run in World Series history, bottom of the ninth inning, first game of the World Series on October 15, 1988. It certainly was, and still is, the most famous home run in Los Angeles Dodgers history. I was only seven years old at the time, and I clearly remember sitting with my mother, father and two brothers in front of our ancient but serviceable television set. The image of Gibson hobbling up to the plate in obvious pain; almost falling on the first swing; quickly falling behind no balls and two strikes; battling back; fouling off pitches and taking the count full; and with one swing writing his name in the history books.

SHE IIIIIIS GONE!

I loved baseball and those guys, major league ball players, were my heroes. Growing up, all I wanted was to be a major league ball player. There was only one problem with that grand ambition. Simply put, I couldn't play worth a lick. In high school I settled for covering sporting events as a reporter for the school newspaper. In college I majored in sports journalism, eventually earning a degree and landing a job at a small neighborhood newspaper in Southern California covering the sports beat.

> *"And look who's coming up! All year long they looked to him to light the fire and all year long he answered the demands until he was physically unable to start tonight. With two bad legs, a bad left hamstring, and a swollen right knee."*
>
> -Vin Scully
> -October 15, 1988

It was in that capacity, as a reporter, that I got to interview one of my childhood heroes, when Kirk Gibson was in town. He was working as a commentator for the Detroit Tigers and the team was in town for a series against the Angels. We sat down over lunch and had a very nice conversation. I asked him about his battle with Parkinson's disease, which he had been diagnosed with in 2015. We talked about the current crop of young ball players coming to the big leagues. Of course, we talked about the Dodgers and the unbelievable season they were having this year, 2017. And we talked about his playing days. I mentioned the autographed poster I still had (somewhere) and how I had seen that at bat, lasting over nine minutes, at least a couple of hundred times. Towards the end of the interview, I asked him about that home run. More specifically, the ball. Where was it? Cooperstown in the Hall of Fame I bet.

"You know," he replied conspiratorially, a smile playing across his face, "it's a funny thing but I don't know where that ball is. As far as I know, no one knows where it is. In all the excitement nobody thought to go find it and no one ever came forward with it. A few months later I got a letter with a photograph from a young woman. In the picture she had a badly bruised thigh where the ball supposedly hit her but that's all I've ever heard about it."

That interview got me thinking. Where was that ball? Why had no one ever come forward with it? If for no other reason than the price it would bring as a collectible. The more I thought about it the more curious I became. If nothing else, the mystery of the missing ball might make a good story. I looked at old film footage of the home run. There was a quick shot, lasting all of about two seconds of the right field pavilion as the ball sailed into the mass of screaming fans. After that, the cameras were all trained on the drama on the playing field as Gibson gamely ran-limped around the base paths, famously pumping his right arm as the entire team charged out of the dugout to mob him at home plate.

On a whim, I called Gibson a few weeks later. I explained that I was doing a story on the ball and did he by any chance still have that letter and photograph? As it turned out he did. It took him awhile to find them, but he soon emailed me copies of both. The woman's name was Harriet Bird. Unfortunately, she no longer lived at the address on the letter. It took me several days of research to track her down but hey, that's what we reporters do, right?

> *"And with two outs you talk about a roll of the dice, this is it! If he hits the ball on the ground, I would imagine he would be running at fifty percent to first base. So the Dodgers trying to catch lightning right now!"*
>
> -Vin Scully
> -October 15, 1988

When finally, I managed to contact her, I asked about that famous home run ball. "Oh yeah, I was there," she replied, "and I had the bruises to prove it. When it happened I lost sight of the ball but I knew from the way the crowd was acting it was a home run. I turned to ask Jack, he was my boyfriend at the time, if he saw where the ball went when suddenly, WHAM, it slams into my hip. I bruise real easy an' that thing hurt like a son of a bitch."

"What happened to the ball after that," I asked?

"Oh people was looking around to see where it went but Jack snatched it up before anyone else could. He had it for a while. Used to keep it on his desk at work. Claimed it was lucky. Until someone stole it." She thought that was very funny and let out a sharp bark of laughter.

"You happen to know how I can reach Jack?" I asked.

"Oh hell, hon. We broke up about a year or so later. Haven't heard from him in years.

He used to work for Hudson Motors in the Valley selling cars. Might still work there for all I know." I thanked her and had the number for Hudson Motors on my laptop before I hung up. This trail was going on twenty-nine years and cold as February in Connecticut, but it was starting to warm up. Maybe I'd get lucky with Hudson.

> *"Fouled away! He was complaining about the fact that, with his left knee bothering him, he can't push off. Well now we can't push off and he can't land."*
>
> -Vin Scully
> -October 15, 1988

I did get lucky. Not only did Jack still work there but he actually answered the phone with a hearty "Hudson Motors, Jack Fisher speaking." He had that breezy, happy-go-lucky voice of an experienced salesman.

After introducing myself, I told him I was a reporter, and I was writing a newspaper story about the home run ball Gibson had hit in the '88 World Series. I explained that it was my understanding that he had the ball. Or at least he had it at one time.

He was only too happy to share on one condition, "call me Pop," he said, and I could hear the wry smile in his gravelly voice. "Nobody calls me Jack anymore," he continued. "It's just Pop Fisher. Yeah, I'll never forget that night. I'm a huge Dodgers fan and tickets to the first game of the World Series, well it doesn't get much better than that. When Gibby hit that ball, I never lost sight of it. I watched it coming down and was reaching for it. I wasn't quite fast enough, and it hit Harriet on the upper thigh. I got lucky because it bounced off her leg straight down into the concrete. Then it bounced straight back up practically into my hands."

"Why didn't you take it down to the clubhouse and give it to Gibson," I asked. "I'm sure he probably would have given you just about anything you asked for."

"Well, I planned to. You know what it was like at the stadium that night?"

"I can imagine."

"No, you really can't. People were going nuts. I mean it was just the first game of the series, but you would think we'd just won game seven. This was baseball history, and everyone knew it. Everyone wanted to stay and soak in the moment. They wanted to be a part of it. I tried to get to the clubhouse, but it was a solid wall of people.

"I finally had to give up. I figured I'd wait a couple of days. Maybe call the Dodger front office and tell them what I had. Get a signed jersey in exchange. Maybe tickets to another World Series game or a couple of games the next season. And to be perfectly honest, I wanted to bring it to work and show some of the guys. Everyone had seen the home run on TV, and I had THAT ball. I mean this was seriously cool."

"So, what made you change your mind?"

"Superstition. I know it sounds kinda lame, but I played some ball in school. Wasn't bad either. Had a couple scouts at least glance in my direction. And you know us ball players, we're some of the most superstitious folks God put on this Earth. Anyway, my playing career never amounted to much. It's a cliché but in my case it rings true… I could never lay off the curve ball."

There was a long pause. He was silent for so long I had to ask if he was still on the line. "Oh yeah. Sorry," he sighed a little as he snapped out of his reverie. "That was twenty-nine years ago. Have some great memories of those days. My life really changed after that night. Anyway, you wanted to know about the ball Gibson hit. I was all of twenty-four back then. I had this job selling cars that I didn't particularly like, and I wasn't particularly good at. Same job I have today. Funny how your perspective can change with time. My personal life was a mess. Harriet and I always seemed to be fighting about one thing or another. I was not in the best of places in those days. I brought the ball in to work on Monday and passed it around and suddenly I was the coolest guy in town. A real celebrity." He laughed at that. "Anyway, I bought one of those clear plastic cubes to protect it and sat it on my desk. That afternoon a gentleman comes in and I happened to be the salesman on the floor. He wanted to buy some vehicles for his business. I showed him a few and we went back to my desk to discuss numbers. Up to that point I don't think he was overly impressed. Whether in me or the vehicles themselves I'm not sure but, like I said, I wasn't very good at the job.

"He sees that ball on my desk and his whole attitude changes. You know the ball had '1988 World Series' printed on it in red ink. Turns out he's a huge Dodgers fan and we spend the next hour talking baseball. He even offered to buy the ball, but I didn't want to sell it. I was still planning on returning it to Gibson at that point. Anyway, before he leaves, he buys twelve new vehicles for his fleet. I was the top salesman that month. And for the next four months in a row.

"After that it seemed like my whole life was changing for the better. I was definitely feeling better about the job and, by extension, feeling better about myself. And even though we broke up the following summer, my relationship with Harriet improved to the point we briefly were talking about marriage. Being a superstitious ex ball player, I really believed it was the ball. I was so convinced that I decided to hang on to it rather than return it to Gibson. I used to keep it on my desk as a good luck charm."

"You really think it was the ball that was responsible for all of that, Pop" I asked?

"Well, I have to admit, it does sound kind of ridiculous now. I mean it was just a happy coincidence that guy walking in when he did. As for the rest of it, I was just feeling more self-confident. The ball didn't do that. I've been with Hudson for almost thirty years. In sixteen of those I was the top salesman for the year. In fact, the ball has been long gone most of those years. And even though I never married Harriet I did meet a great gal a couple of years later and we have two great kids. The ball didn't do any of that either. I don't know. Maybe the ball just nudged me in the right direction," he laughed again.

"You said the ball was long gone. What happened to it?"

"Stolen. Like I said, I kept it on my desk for luck. Got to be a joke around here. Any time I sold a car everyone would say 'Hey, Gibson just sold another car.' I had it for almost a year then one day the following summer I came to work, and it was gone."

"And you never knew who took it." It was more of a statement than a question. I had a sinking feeling my story would end here.

"Never said that! I knew exactly who took it! Well...I could never prove it and he flat out denied it, but I'm probably ninety per cent certain it was Walter Whambold. He used to work here back in the day. Fact is he was the top salesman before I hit my hot streak. That never sat well with him. Probably didn't help that every time I sold a car, I'd take that ball out of its' plastic case and rub it for luck. And I made sure he saw me do it too. So, in a way, I probably deserved that.

"Anyway, if that ball was lucky, it wasn't lucky for old Walter. Few weeks after it went missing, he was taking a test drive with a customer and the guy runs a light and gets T-boned on the passenger side. Messed Walter up pretty bad."

"You wouldn't, by any chance, know how I could get in touch with Walter, would you Pop," I asked and then held my breath?

"Matter of fact I do. One of the guys has been here longer than I have. He and Walter still keep in touch. I think they play poker a couple times a month. Let me see if I can get his number for ya."

> *"4 to 3 A's. Two out, ninth inning, not a bad opening act. Mike Davis, by the way, has stolen 7 out of 10 if you're wondering about Lasorda throwing the dice again. Oh and one! Fouled away again!"*
>
> -Vin Scully
> -October 15, 1988

I heard the click-clack of a keyboard and let out my breath as Jack read the number to me. So far so good I thought to myself. Of course, I had no way of knowing if Walter was really involved with the stolen ball but Pop sure thought he was. Even if he was the culprit, he may not be willing to own up to it. But any lead is a good lead, and I dialed the number Pop had given me. Walter Whambold answered right away. He had a raspy, sandpapery voice gained from too many years smoking unfiltered cigarettes. He probably smoked Camels like my dad. Both had that roughness in their voice that made every syllable sound like it was being dragged through thorn bushes. After introducing myself, I was relieved to discover he had read a couple of my articles in the newspaper and was something of a fan. Score one for the reporter. Even so, he was, at first, reluctant to talk about what had happened. Finally, after some gentle prodding, he opened up to me.

"Hell, it was what, thirty years ago. I suppose even if he wanted to make an issue outta it the statue of limitations ran out." He mispronounced statute. Most people do and, as someone who writes for a living, it irritates the heck out of me. I bit my tongue and let him continue. "Yeah, I stole his damn ball. The day he brought that thing in he thought he was something special. Truth is he was just a pissant, snot nosed kid that thought he could sell cars. I really got tired of his attitude and needed to bring him down a peg or two. And the way he'd go on about that ball being the Kirk Gibson home run ball and it being lucky. I never bought that for a second. He bought that at a souvenir stand and tried to pass it off. If it was the real deal he'd a sold it for a small fortune.

I'm sure someone woulda paid good money for that ball...if it was legit, which it wasn't." Walter seemed to be a very angry man.

"So, what did you do with the ball," I asked politely, trying not to get drawn into his tirade?

"I knew he'd figure it was me stole the damn thing. I didn't wanna have it when he came lookin', which he did. I left it with my ma. Figured he'd never think to look there, and he didn't. I figured I'd wait a few months and then sell it. If he could convince those yahoos at Hudson that it was the Kirk Gibson ball, I'm sure I could sell it to some schnook!

"Lucky ball my ass," he grumbled under his breath. "Never brought me any luck. You know a few weeks after all that went down, I was out with a customer doing a test drive and this ass hole decides to run a red light. Got T-boned by a pick-up truck. Damn near died. Was in the hospital for over a month and laid up for close to a year after that. I still walk with a limp. After that I never wanted to see that ball again. Told my ma to keep it."

"So, you think it was the ball that caused the accident?"

"What! No!" he replied, his voice rising. "I just...well I was just done with it see."

"So, do you know if your mom still has that ball? Can I get in touch with her?"

"No, ma died back in '98. Her younger sister, my aunt Iris, still lives in Ma's house though. She might know where it is. You think that ball mighta been the real deal?"

"Probably not," I fibbed. I'm not sure why I lied, but Walter Whambold didn't seem to be the type of man I wanted to trust. "Even if it was, there's really no way to prove it, especially after almost thirty years," I finished truthfully. "One last question," I said on an odd impulse.   "Do you happen to recall the date of your accident?"

"Never forget it. It was October 15, 1989. Is that important?"

"Not really."

"Oh and one! Fouled away again!"

-Vin Scully
-October 15, 1988

MAKING CONTACT WITH THE COUNT FULL

Walter gave me a number where I could reach Iris Gaines, his aunt. He also gave me an address and, as it was in the area, I decided to chance an unannounced visit. The house I pulled up to was in a well-to-do part of town. It was an old Victorian, built not long after the turn of the last century. It was two stories with a buttressed and steepled roof supported on ornate, hand carved columns. Peering from between the columns, like opalescent eyes, were two large plate glass windows gazing out over a beautifully manicured lawn. The woman that answered the door was hardly what I expected. First, I was talking about events from twenty-nine years ago. Even though I hadn't met the man, the math put Walter in his mid-fifties at least, and probably north of sixty. His cauterized voice sure sounded the part. Iris Gaines was a tall, statuesque woman with piercing gray eyes, an aquiline nose, and close-cropped blonde hair. At first, I placed her at around sixty, but she had a dazzling smile accentuated by high cheek bones that immediately made her appear ten years younger.

I explained I was trying to track down a baseball from the 1988 World Series and Walter, her nephew, may have left it here once upon a time. She didn't ask and I didn't feel the need to mention exactly what ball it was, simply that it was a memento that had turned up missing and I was writing a human-interest piece for the newspaper. She was very cordial and invited me in, offering me a bottle of water as I settled into a comfortably overstuffed sofa that was probably as old as the house.

"Why yes, I do remember that baseball," she said in a Jessica Rabbit voice as she settled in convivially next to me. I caught the scent of her perfume, and it made my head swim faintly. "Well, it might not be the same ball, I mean one baseball looks pretty much like another now, doesn't it?" She laughed a sultry, yet lighthearted tune and her eyes sparkled. I don't know what it was about Iris, but I was thoroughly smitten. I don't think it was me either, as I imagine she had this effect on all men. Just something about the woman oozed sexuality.

"My sister, that's Walter's mother, was much older than I. When she became ill, I moved in here to help take care of her for the final few years of her life. Lord knows Walter wasn't about to take on that kind of responsibility. It really was a godsend for me. I'd spent most of my life tramping around without any permanent address to speak of, so moving here gave me a sense of, I guess stability is as good a word as any. My sister passed in the fall of '98, poor thing. Because of the age difference we were never particularly close growing up. I mean when I was in grade school she had already moved out of the house and was starting a family of her own. Did you know I'm only two years older than Walter? He's always been more like a cousin than a nephew. Anyway, sis and I did become close those last few years. I really felt like I had a sister for once. When she passed, she left the house to me, which pissed Walter off no end.

"Anyway, I had a hard time letting go. I mean in my mind it was still her house and all her belongings. So, it was close to a year before I decided that it was time. I had a big yard sale, everything must go sort of thing. I was cleaning out the attic and I came across this box of odds and ends and I remember seeing the ball in there. I remember it partly because of the big red 1988 World Series written on it but it also struck me as odd since my sister didn't know a thing about the game. I called Walter, thinking it may have been his, and that was the other odd thing I remembered. He told me to get whatever I could for it and to keep the money."

"You wouldn't happen to remember who bought it, would you," I asked.

"Actually, I do! It was little Bobby Savoy. His family used to live just down the street. They moved about ten years ago. Don't know where he is now."

"One last question. You said your sister died in the fall. If you don't mind my asking, what day did she pass?"

"Why it was October 15. October 15, 1998."

I thanked Iris and told her she had been a tremendous help. I hadn't asked but as I walked back to my car, I thought I could put money on October 15, 1999, as the date little Bobby Savoy had purchased that ball at Iris' yard sale.

> *"Oh and two to Gibson. The infield is back with two out and Davis at first. Now Gibson during the year, not necessarily in this spot, but he was a threat to bunt. No way tonight! No wheels!"*
>
> -Vin Scully
> -October 15, 1988

Tracking down Bobby Savoy proved to be remarkably easy. But in this day-and-age with computers, cell phones, and social media, finding anyone isn't all that difficult. He was working as an auto mechanic in the Valley. I called him and asked about the ball, and he remembered it. I felt like I was getting really close and didn't want to have this conversation over the telephone so he suggested that I come by the shop where he worked.

I arrived just as he went on his lunch break. He was thirty-ish, not particularly tall but broad shouldered and muscular, with an unruly mass of dark hair. He spoke in a soft, soprano voice and his words were slow and measured. "I was ten when I bought the ball. It was really just an excuse to talk to Mz. Gaines." He appeared to blush slightly. "Most of the guys in the neighborhood had a thing for her. She was older but real good looking, you know. Couple of the guys dared me to talk to her when she was having this big yard sale. I was just looking for something, anything that I could use as a prop to start a conversation. Then I saw this baseball. It said 1988 World Series in red letters on it. I remember asking her if it was really used in the Series. She said she didn't know but maybe. She was asking five dollars for it, but she said if I wanted it I could have it for two.

"When I got back to my buddies it turned out they were more impressed by the ball. It was totally rad that I had a 1988 World Series baseball, even if it wasn't used in a game. I doubt that it really was used though. I mean it looked brand new." He paused and seemed to turn that statement over in his mind like he had just remembered something important.

I gave him some space and, as realization came over his face, I said "something?"

"I don't know," he replied. "I never really gave it much thought before, but now that I am thinking about it, that ball always looked brand new. And I didn't just put it on a shelf in my room and forget about it either. That next summer I dragged that ball everywhere with me. It was my second year of little league. The summer before I was horrible. So, I used to practice with that ball. I'd hit it off a batting tee for hours. Then I got my dad to slow pitch it to me. I beat the crap out of that thing. You'd think it'd be all scuffed or, at the very least, a couple of stitches would have busted. It's been almost twenty years since I saw it last, but I don't recall any of that. It looked the same as the day Mz. Gaines sold it to me for two dollars."

"Well, did all that extra BP help," I asked?

"Oh yeah. It was like nobody could get me out that season. I led our team in batting average, hits, home runs, RBI's...just about every statistic there was.

"Whatever happened to the baseball," I prodded gently?

"Scotty Carson happened," he retorted, the disdain evident simply by the way he spat the name out like a piece of stale bread. After that he paused for a long while.

"And who...," I pushed gently.

"Is Scotty Carson," he finished my sentence. "Neighborhood bully. Every neighborhood has one. He was a couple years older than we were. Big for his age and, obviously, much bigger than any of us. He jumped me on the way home from practice one afternoon. Punched me and knocked me down. Said he wanted my World Series ball. He knew I always had it with me. Said he wouldn't stop until I gave him the ball... or I was dead. I decided to give it to him."

"You told your parents what happened, didn't you?"

"Oh sure. My dad spoke to Scotty's dad, Gus. Of course, Scotty denied it and his dad sided with Scotty. Wasn't much else we could do. I mean it was only a baseball. Scotty eventually got his though."

"He did? What happened?"

"The baseball and some of the other stuff he pulled, they were just practice. He had a bunch of run ins with the cops not long after that. For a while there it seemed like the police were at his house once or twice a month. Eventually he ended up in jail. Breaking and entering. Burglarizing houses in the neighborhood. He was in and out of jail a few times after that. Mostly in. Last I heard he was doing a long stretch up in Lom Poc. I'm sure I ain't the only one won't shed any tears on account of him."

Bobby paused for a long moment. Then he sighed and, collecting his breath, he continued, "I really felt sorry for his old man, Gus. His dad really wanted to believe the best in Scotty. That's why he always had his back when there were problems in the neighborhood. I ran into Gus a few years later. Or, really, he tracked me down. I was in high school by then. He said he had found out that Scotty had taken my ball, and a bunch of other stuff from kids in the neighborhood and wanted to make amends. Even offered to pay for it. I told him not to sweat it. I only paid two dollars for the ball. The apology was repayment enough."

"Did he say if he knew what happened to the ball?"

"He did. You should probably talk to him about that though. He lives in the same house. I can give you his address."

NOW, IF I CAN JUST MAKE IT AROUND THE BASES

"No balls, two strikes, two out. Little nubber....foul. And it had to be an effort to run that far. Gibson was so banged up he was not introduced. He did not come out onto the field before the game. It's one thing to favor one leg but you can't favor two."

-Vin Scully

-October 15, 1988

I found myself returning to the same neighborhood I had visited when I called on Iris Gaines, this time just a few blocks down the street. When I pulled up outside the house Bobby had directed me to, I didn't get out of my car right away. I needed a few minutes to collect my thoughts. This was very fascinating stuff. First there was a ball that didn't seem to deteriorate no matter the abuse heaped upon it. Then there was certainly a pattern here. Those who came by the ball honestly seemed to be granted good fortune…Pop's transformation into a super car salesman, Iris was left the house that, at some point, was surely intended for Walter, Bobby's little league hot streak.

Those that came by the ball dishonestly seemed to suffer an inordinate amount of bad luck…Walter and his near fatal car accident, and Scotty, it would seem, was not getting out of jail any time soon. I wondered what light Gus might shed on this story.

Gus was probably in his sixties but had a hang dog expression that made him appear much older. Having a jailbird son can do that to a man. His hands shook ever so slightly, and he had the rheumy eyes of someone who spends a great deal of time with a bottle. He seemed sober when we met. Sober and a bit apprehensive when I explained my purpose. His son was already in prison. He didn't need this old baseball story coming back on him. I assured him I was only interested in where the ball was, and I could even leave Scotty's name out of the article. That seemed to allay his concerns somewhat.

"You know I always wanted the best for my boy. I always backed him up when the folks around here accused him of anything. Towards the end though, well you know what they say, where there's smoke..." he trailed off. Like Bobby I felt sorry for Gus. "In 2003 I accidentally came across the World Series ball he stole from the Savoy kid. He'd hidden it in the garage. When I confronted him, he admitted the whole thing. Acted like it was no big deal, but it was a big deal. You know I almost got into a fist fight with Bobby's dad over that ball. When I found it, hidden away in the garage with a bunch of other stuff he had taken from kids in the neighborhood, I felt like such a dammed fool."

"Why didn't you return it?"

He pondered over that question for a moment. "I could lie and say I was worried that my no-good son would just steal it back. That I didn't want to give him a reason to confront Bobby Savoy again, maybe hurt him. And that was part of it I suppose. But the real reason, the main reason was, I was embarrassed. After the way I got into it with Bobby's dad I just couldn't bring myself to admit I was wrong about my son. So, I decided to send that ball as far away as I could. Back then I worked for a financial services company. We were nationwide and had an office in Chicago. There was a guy in Chicago, another broker. We'd never met but we did speak over the phone on a regular basis, usually couple times a week. I'm a big Dodgers fan and he was a Cubs fan, so we were always talking trash to each other, all good natured. I decided to have a little fun, at least make something positive out of the situation. I mailed the ball to him with a note. Something like 'Enjoy this ball. It's about as close as you'll ever get to a World Series.'"

He smiled at the memory as I suppressed a chuckle. "So, any chance he still has it," I asked? "Any way you can put me in touch with him?"

"I don't know if he still has it. You'd have to ask him. That might be a problem though. As a rule, he doesn't talk to reporters."

That certainly piqued my curiosity. "Why not? Who is this guy?"

"You're gonna laugh when I tell you." He paused here for dramatic effect. "It was Steve Bartman."

Yeah, that Steve Bartman. The very same. If you don't know who Steve Bartman is, I have to wonder why you're reading this story. Go ahead and Google him. I'll wait. After that night In Chicago Bartman became a recluse. He changed his phone number and went deep underground. He was notoriously press-shy which, given the circumstances, was understandable. He had passed on five figure deals to make personal appearances, so I doubted my little newspaper story about a missing World Series baseball would offer up much enticement for him to talk to me. Considering all of this, I was fairly certain my search would end here.

But Gus wanted to help. Perhaps he believed in Karma. Maybe he was still trying to make up for the sins of the son. He said, while he was no longer in regular contact with Bartman, he did keep in touch, mostly during the baseball season. He said he needed to call him soon what with the Cubs and Dodgers meeting in the upcoming NLCS. He was more than willing to pass along my contact information and explain why I wanted to speak to him. For my part, all I could do was sit back, cross my fingers, and let Bartman decide for himself if I was worthy. Gus did say Bartman had mellowed somewhat after the Cubs won the Series in 2016 so maybe he'd call me. I could only hope.

> *"Oh and two to Gibson. Ball one. And a throw down to first! Davis just did get back. Good play by Ron Hassey using Gibson as a screen. He took a shot at the runner and Mike Davis didn't see it for that split second and that made it close."*
>
> -Vin Scully
>
> -October 15, 1988

I was tantalizingly close to solving the puzzle, and I won't deny that the story and Bartman's connection to it weighed upon my mind. Mercifully, I did not have to agonize for very long. A couple of days later I received a telephone call. I didn't recognize the number, but it was a Chicago area code causing me to almost fall backwards out of my chair. I held my breath as I answered.

"This is Steve Bartman," a disembodied voice issued haltingly from my too tightly grasped iPhone. "I understand you wanted to speak to me about the baseball Gus Carson gave me back in 2003?"

"Yes sir, Mr. Bartman," I replied, probably a little too eagerly. "I appreciate your taking the time to call me. I know you don't generally do interviews."

"Well, I almost didn't call." He paused and when he continued, he seemed a little more at ease. "It was such an odd request, though. Everyone always wants to talk about that day and frankly, it's a day I've tried my best to forget. But all you want is to talk about a 1988 World Series baseball that I once owned for a very brief time. So, I'm glad to answer any questions about that ball, but if you start talking about that game I'm hanging up. Understood?"

"Yes sir," I replied, trying to hide the disappointment in my voice upon hearing the words 'once owned'. That meant, while I was one step closer, I had not quite reached the end of the story just yet.

"Fine," his tone brightened even more. "And call me Steve. Mr. Bartman was my father." He laughed at his cliched joke. "Before we start, though, I do have one question for you. What's so special about that baseball?"

I had to stop and consider that for a moment. Aside from Pop and Walter, I hadn't told anyone the true nature of the ball. And they had both known the history behind it anyway. I hadn't lied to anyone. I simply introduced myself by saying I was writing a human-interest story about this baseball memento that went missing, which was true. No one had asked me directly about the ball...until Steve Bartman. It's not that I wanted to find the ball and claim it for myself either. Sure, it would be a super cool memento but there was no way to authenticate it. I just wanted the story which, in my mind, was way cooler. I was more worried that if someone knew what the ball was, they might get the idea they could make some money off it and shut down on me. That's just my cynical nature at work though.

I weighed my moral code and my journalists' ethics against getting the story at all costs. In the end it really wasn't close. Besides, I liked Steve Bartman. He seemed like a good guy that had had a lot thrown at him. He'd kept his dignity throughout, and he still lived in Chicago. Now that took guts. He also didn't strike me as the type to covet the ball and try to make a quick buck from it. So, I told Steve the whole story. When I was finished, he began to laugh. It started as a little snicker but quickly progressed into a full blown, belly busting, gale of laughter. I didn't get the joke, so I patiently waited for him to get ahold of himself.

When the laughter had subsided, I could almost picture him leaning back and wiping tears from his eyes, he had laughed so long and hard. "I'm sorry," he said the laughter still in his voice. "I haven't had a good laugh like that in I don't know how long. I don't usually believe in things like curses but after that night in 2003, let's just say I'm more open-minded about certain possibilities. If this was the Kirk Gibson ball, then I guess even it wasn't powerful enough to break the Cubs Curse. At least it sure didn't do any favors for me. I was laughing at the absurd irony of it all. At least the Cubs organization was always very sympathetic to what had happened, making it clear they, in no way, held me responsible. They kept tabs on me and made sure I was okay both physically and mentally. Here I am breaking my own rule and talking about that day."

"But you said that you didn't have the ball for very long," I interjected, gently steering him back on track as we reporters are wont to do.

"Well, I got the ball in the mail, along with Gus Carson's note, a few days before that game. I had the ball with me that night, fifteen years to the day that Gibson hit his homer. Now I've got a good sense of humor and Gus and I were always doing stuff like that during the season. We'd never met but we were both big baseball fans. After that night the joke didn't seem so funny anymore. I'm sure you know I had to be escorted out of the stadium after the game by security guards for my own protection. They handed me off to the Chicago PD who escorted me home. The cops even staked out my house for about a month. I was getting death threats until I changed my number. There was this one cop who was especially helpful. A big red headed Irishman named

Red Blow. Nicest guy you could ever meet. When I got home that night, I thanked him. All of a sudden baseball wasn't fun anymore, so I reached into my pocket and pulled out that ball and gave it to him. In that moment it was the last thing I wanted.

"Red was one of the cops assigned to watch my house. He and I kept in touch even after things settled down. About six months later he was shot while on the job. The Chicago PD took him off active duty and gave him a desk job. That lasted about a year. He'd been shot in the lower back and there were still fragments in there. Sitting in a chair all day he began having back problems, probably related to the fragments. The force eventually mustered him out on early retirement and disability. Got a big cash settlement out of the deal too."

"You two still keep in touch," I asked?

"Well, here's some good news for you. Yes, we do keep in touch. He hated the Chicago winters, so he sold his house and used the money from the settlement to buy a house in a warmer climate, out your way, down in San Diego. Even better, I can't say for sure but I'm ninety percent certain he still has your ball. Leastways he did about three years ago when I visited him."

Steve was more than willing to share Red's phone number, for which I thanked him profusely. This might have been the best news I had heard yet. I didn't hesitate and immediately called Red in San Diego. Somewhat out of breath, I hastily explained I was a friend of Steve's, and could I interview Red the following morning for a story I was working on? I could have done it right then and there on the telephone, but I was so close to the end of the story that I really wanted to do the interview in person. Especially if he had the ball. Up until now, Gibson's ball was almost like a Unicorn. If it did still exist, I really wanted to see it up close and personal. Maybe even touch it. What is it Sam Spade says in The Maltese Falcon? "It's the stuff dreams are made of." Talk about life imitating art. That line really struck home. And Red was only too happy for the company, so I agreed to meet him at his home the next morning.

> *"There goes Davis and it's fouled away! So Mike Davis, who had stolen seven out of ten and carrying the tying run, was on the move."*
>
> -Vin Scully
> -October 15, 1988

That day was to be a busy and an extremely memorable day as well. Not only did I have a morning interview with one Red Blow, but I would need to hightail it about one hundred twenty miles back up the freeway to conduct pregame interviews with the home team as the Dodgers were playing the Cubs in the NLCS that evening. The irony of it all was not lost on me.

With this in mind, I arrived at Red's front door promptly at ten AM. I was greeted by a large, bear of a red headed, Irishman. In addition to the fire on top, he also sported a flowing red beard streaked throughout with white. There was a certain twinkle in his eye and a mischievous smile set upon his face and I thought that, perhaps in another life, he may have been Santa Claus. He was dressed in gray sweatpants and a matching hoodie. Upon seeing me he laughed and took my hand in one of his meaty paws and began pumping it vigorously as he pulled me into his cozy little home. As he did this, he said in a great baritone voice "pleased to make your acquaintance son. Any friend of Steve Bartmans' is a friend of mine," laughing as he did so. He waved me into a lived-in sitting room, grabbed a cane, and cautiously followed me. After offering me a seat on an overstuffed sofa, he eased into the recliner across from me.

He settled into the recliner facing me, looked me in the eye, smiled knowingly, and said "of course you're not exactly a friend of Steves' now are ya son?"

The question caught me completely off guard. I had only said I was a friend to avoid a lot of explanation over the phone. Even though I fully intended to explain my relationship to Steve, Red had beaten me to it and caught me in a lie, albeit of the white variety. This was not a good way to start.

I sat there hemming and hawing, beneath Reds' discerning gaze, unable to find the necessary words. Imagine that. Finally, he broke the silence as his face split into a wide grin. "'Saw right," he said, amused by my discomfort. "Just remember son,

33

never lie to a cop. Even an ex-cop." He laughed, making me think of Santa Clause once again. I had the feeling Red spent a great deal of his day laughing both at, and with, those around him.

"I called Steve to check out your bonafides. Force of habit," he frowned. It seemed an expression unaccustomed to his face. "He said you're alright. That's good 'nuff for me. Said you were interested in the baseball he gave me the night that...well, you know."

"Yeah," I replied as I breathed a huge sigh of relief. "Steve told me the last time he was here you still had it," I said, leaning forward in anticipation.

"And I still do. Care to see it?"

My jaw dropped and I almost rolled forward and off the sofa when I heard that. Somehow, I managed to keep my cool and answered, "only if it's not any trouble."

"None at all, son. Back in a flash with the cash." Leaning on the cane, he rose stiffly to his feet. I noticed he winced as he reached his full height. "Guess Steve told ya I was shot in the line of duty a few years back," he said over his shoulder as he shuffled into the adjoining dining room. "Really did a number on my back. Some days are better than others. This is not starting out to be a good day," he said as he opened a glass curio cabinet. "Was worse when I lived in Chicago" he continued, idly pulling a pair of objects from the case. I may have drooled slightly.

> *"Gibson shaking his left leg making it quiver. Like a horse trying to get rid of a troublesome fly. Two and two. Mike Scioscia can only sit now and sweat it out. He led off the inning and popped up."*

-Vin Scully

-October 15, 1988

TINKER BELL TAKE A SEAT

I couldn't believe it. I had been hot on the trail of this thing for the better part of two weeks, to the point of obsession. I wasn't even sure the ball still existed. And now I might finally have found it. Red shuffled back into the room, leaning heavily on his cane, something cradled in the crook of his free arm. I jumped up off the sofa to help him with his burden. "Thanks son," he rasped. "Getting old ain't for pussies." He barked laughter and seemed more his cheerful self as he settled back into the recliner. A coffee table sat before the sofa and I placed two clear plastic cubes, each containing a baseball, upon it between the two of us. I stared at the one which rested slightly closer to Red. The stitching looked brand new. Lettered in red ink were the words 'Official Ball 1988 World Series' with Commissioner Peter Ueberroths' signature scrawled beneath that. My unblinking gaze was fixated on that ball.

"You wanna hold it son," asked Red as he used the tip of his cane to push the cube in my direction?

Would I! I carefully lifted the box, turning it this way and that as I held it up to the light. I examined it from all angles. I wanted desperately to open the box and touch the ball but was unsure of the proper etiquette in this situation.

Finally Red asked "I thought you wanted to hold it?"

When all he got for reply was a blank stare he boomed "take it outta the box, son," and laughed heartily.

As I reverently took the ball from its case Red asked, "what is so damn special about that ball, anyway?"

Not taking my eyes from the ball I replied, "Steve didn't tell you?"

"He said you'd been tracking it as a lost souvenir or somethin'. Said if I wanted to know any more, I'd have to ask you. So, I'm askin'" he laughed.

For a second time I considered the merits of lying. I could offer to buy the ball from Red and probably get it cheap. But then what. First, even if I had the ball there's no way I could ever prove it was The ball. I knew in my heart it was, but I doubt I'd be able to convince anyone else, much less get MLB to validate it. And, heck, all I ever wanted was the story and now I had that. The ball, at this point, was immaterial. Besides, Red had already caught me in one lie. I figured he'd know if I was lying again. And then there was the fact that everyone that had come into possession of the ball dishonestly had had bad luck. Color me superstitious.

So, I told Red the whole story, beginning to end, along with my (only slightly) crazy theory that the ball brought luck, both good and bad depending on how you obtained it. He listened intently, leaning forward on his ever-present cane as I spoke. After I finished, he sat back in his chair, a meaty hand stroking his beard. "That's a hell of a story there son. And you say there's no way to authenticate the ball one way or t'other?"

"None that I'm aware of, Red."

He paused for a long while, hand still stroking his beard. When at last he spoke his words almost caused me to fall off the sofa a second time. "You want it," he asked?

Keeping cool I responded, "It's a generous offer but I just came here for a story," "Sure ya did, son. But you and I both know you want the ball too. Take it. It's yours. Besides, I have this which is far more valuable to me." With that he leaned forward and snatched up the second box from the table.

Looking closely, I could see a ball similar to mine but with the words 'Official Ball 2016 World Series' written on it. And where the ball I held in my hands was unmarked this one was smudged. No, not smudged, signed. Covered by more than a dozen signatures, many overlapping one another.

"I still had friends on the force in Chicago. If there was one thing I did miss about Chicago it was my Cubs. Usually catch at least a couple of games when they're here in town. Anyway, I managed to wrangle a ticket for game 7. Afterwards I bought this souvenir ball and got most of the players to sign it. They'll bury me with this. Ha," he barked, and I smiled but before I could begin to laugh at his joke, he looked me in the eye sternly. "I'm dead serious son. It's in the will." He laughed again and I didn't know if he was serious or not. I guess that was the point. So, I just laughed with him.

"Regarding your ball there," he said, gesturing towards the ball I still clutched tightly, "I've given it some thought, and it seems whoever gets the ball honestly," and he stressed the word honestly, "gets whatever they desire most. Pop Fisher seemed to just want some happiness in his life. Sounds like he got that. Iris Gaines wanted a place of her own. Done! Little Bobby Savoy got to be the star of his little league team. What kid doesn't want that? Even our friend Steve Bartman got lucky. It just took a bit longer what with the Curse and all. You know the Cubs gave him an honorary 2016 World Series ring. Just to show there were no hard feelings and they didn't hold him responsible for what happened. It's his most prized possession and I imagine they'll bury it with him also." He laughed again.

"What did you get," I asked, eying the cane?

"You're lookin' at it," he said holding up the baseball, still in its case. "I also think it's just one wish to a customer. I got mine so now it's someone else's turn. Might as well be you."

Looking down at the ball I said, "You sure there's any magic left in this thing?" I chuckled softly as I turned it over in my hand. "Seems like it's granted a lot of wishes. That and beating the Curse probably took a lot out of it."

"Well, it's been sitting on a shelf in my bedroom for fourteen years. It's probably like a battery, recharging itself. Must have a full charge after all that time."

I squinted my eyes looking at the ball in wonder, as I slowly rotated it in my hand. "You really think so?"

"I have no fucking idea," he laughed. "We're talking about a freaking magic baseball. It didn't come with an instruction manual."

I looked at the time, almost eleven o'clock. The game that night started at five with the press allowed in to talk to the players at two. With traffic, I probably had just enough time to make the stadium by then. I thanked Red, pocketed the ball, and jumped into my car for the long drive back to LA.

> *"Two balls and two strikes with two out! There he goes. Way outside. He's stolen it! So Mike Davis, the tying run, is at second base with two out. Now the Dodgers don't need the muscle of Gibson as much as a base hit. And on deck is the leadoff man, Steve Sax."*
>
> -Vin Scully
> -October 15, 1988

I managed to pull into the stadium parking lot with time to spare. My editor probably didn't get my best work that night. I did the requisite interviews with different players, but my mind kept drifting to the bulge in the pocket of my wind breaker. I was interviewing Justin Turner when something clicked. Red had said the ball granted your heart's desire. The only thing I had wanted these past few weeks was this story, the story of what happened to Gibson's home run ball. I had that. My wish was granted. And I suddenly realized it was October 15…again. That had to mean something. Where this ball was concerned this was a very special day.

Much like Kirk Gibson in 1988 Justin Turner was, in many ways, the heart and soul of this team. I reached into my pocket and pulled out the ball. Justin glanced down at what I was holding. "Whatcha got there," he asked?

"It's a good luck charm," I replied. "At least it seems to bring luck to those that have it.

I want you to have it."

"You sure man? That's a 1988 World Series ball. It must be valuable."

"Naw," I lied casually. "Just a souvenir ball. But it does represent the '88 Series, last time you guys were there. Take it. Maybe it will bring you some luck."

> *"Three and two! Sax waiting on deck, but the game right now is at the plate. High fly ball into right field. She iiiiiis gone! In a year that has been so improbable, the impossible has happened. And now the only question was could he make it around the base paths unassisted."*
>
> -Vin Scully
> -October 15, 1988

Well JT took that ball on the night of October 15, 2017. It was twenty-nine years to the day since Gibson hit his famous home run. And if you know your baseball history you know that Turner hit a walk off three-run home run that night to beat the Cubs and put the Dodgers up two games to none.

I would have liked to talk to him that night, myself and every reporter on the planet. I decided to give him his moment. I was far more interested in going home and writing the story of Gibby's Ball. But the story needed a proper ending, a proper resting place for the ball. The next day was a travel day for the team. I contacted the team press secretary and called in a favor or two and got JT on the phone. I had decided to tell him about the history behind the ball. He might not believe it. Hell, if I hadn't heard the stories with my own ears, I probably wouldn't believe it. But at least he could make an informed decision about what to do with the ball.

"You know, I said it once before a few days ago that Kirk Gibson was not the most valuable player. That the most valuable player for the Dodgers was Tinkerbell. But tonight I think Tinkerbell backed off for Kirk Gibson."

-Vin Scully

-October 15, 1988

When he came on the phone I said "congratulations! Great game last night!"

"Thanks man. I'm still riding this incredible high and haven't come down yet. The whole team is stoked. Surprised I didn't see you last night."

"Well, I figured the last thing you wanted was to talk to another reporter. Figured I'd let you enjoy your moment. Besides, I had a deadline. Guess that ball I gave you was lucky after all."

"Oh yeah, the ball. Yeah, maybe it was."

"You have it with you?" I was feeling somehow protective of it.

"Oh shoot! I sure hope you didn't want it back!"

"No, no," I said, trying to hide the mounting concern in my voice. "I gave it to you to keep."

"Oh man. I'm really sorry. I don't have it." A silence filled the air as I waited for him to continue. "The, ahh, fan that caught my ball. He came to the clubhouse after the game to return it. It was funny. He said that ball was really important to him. I said it was kind of important to me also. Told him he could have whatever he wanted. Only trouble was he didn't know what he wanted. I told him to think about it and when he figured it out to get back to me. We were standing next to my locker and the ball you gave me was right there. I pulled it out and said 'until then, I'll trade ya.'"

"So, he has the ball. You know how to get in touch with him?"

"No. But I'm sure he'll get in touch as soon as he figures out what he wants. You want me to ask him to call you?"

I thought about that for a second. "No. In a way it's fitting. Let him keep it."

I wished him luck in Chicago and disconnected. I sat in a long silence, thinking of the irony. A silence broken by the ring tone of my cell phone. When I answered I recognized the unmistakable baritone laughter of one Red Blow. "You gave Turner the ball, didn't you," he snorted?

"Yeah, I did."

"Well, dammit all to hell," he laughed again? "I knew it. The minute he hit that ball I knew it. I gave you the ball. I never expected you'd use it agin me," he began laughing again.

As soon as he had himself under control, he asked me where the ball was. I repeated what JT had told me. "And you don't know who the fan is," Red asked.

"Nope! And I don't want to know. That ball, it doesn't want to be found. I think, for whatever reason, it let me find it. Then it chose to disappear again. Best to let sleeping dogs lie. Never understood that saying until right now."

"I think you're probably right. But someone out there is about to get very lucky." Red was still laughing as I disconnected.

> *Authors note: The above story is obviously a work of fiction. All good historical fiction has a kernel of truth…or two. To date the ball that Kirk Gibson hit into the right field bleachers on the night of October 15, 1988 has never been returned. Gibson has said a woman sent him a picture of her bruised thigh where that ball hit her. So those two simple facts inspired this story. For you purists, before you start sending me angry letters, I know the Steve Bartman incident took place on October 14, not the 15th as stated in the story. I cite poetic license to change the date. It makes for a better story.*

HISTORY IS BEING WRITTEN

Printed in the United States
by Baker & Taylor Publisher Services